Está lloviendo
It's Raining

Celeste Bishop

traducido por / translated by
Charlotte Bockman

ilustrado por / illustrated by
Maria José Da Luz

PowerKiDS
press™

New York

Published in 2017 by The Rosen Publishing Group, Inc.
29 East 21st Street, New York, NY 10010

First Edition

Managing Editor: Nathalie Beullens-Maoui
Editor: Sarah Machajewski
Book Design: Michael Flynn
Spanish Translator: Charlotte Bockman
Illustrator: Maria José Da Luz

Cataloging-in-Publication Data

Names: Bishop, Celeste.
Title: It's raining = Está lloviendo / Celeste Bishop.
Description: New York : Powerkids Press, 2016. | Series: What's the weather like? = ¿Qué tiempo hace? | In English and Spanish. | Includes index.
Identifiers: ISBN 9781499423075 (library bound)
Subjects: LCSH: Rain and rainfall–Juvenile literature. | Weather–Juvenile literature.
Classification: LCC QC924.7 B57 2016 | DDC 551.57'7–dc23

Manufactured in the United States of America

CPSIA Compliance Information: Batch #BS16PK: For Further Information contact Rosen Publishing, New York, New York at 1-800-237-9932

Contenido

Contents

Oigo golpecitos en la ventana de mi cuarto.

I hear tapping on my bedroom window.

4

¡Está lloviendo!

It's raining!

La lluvia viene de las nubes en el cielo.

Rain comes from the clouds in the sky.

Las gotas de lluvia pueden ser grandes o pequeñas.

Raindrops can be big or small.

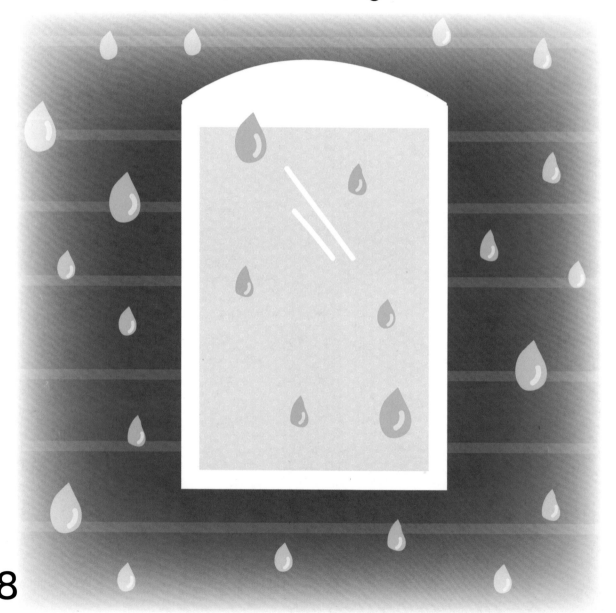

Hacen que todo se moje.

They make everything wet.

9

No puedo salir cuando llueve. Juego dentro.

I can't go outside when it's raining. I play inside.

11

Mi hermano y yo hacemos una fortaleza
en su cuarto.

My brother and I make a fort in his room.

Usamos muchas almohadas.

We use lots of pillows.

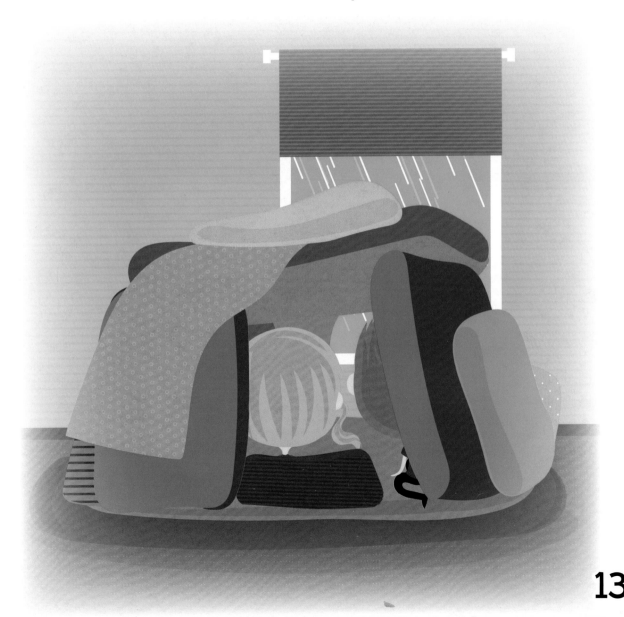

Nos imaginamos que nuestra fortaleza
es un barco pirata. ¡Llueve en alta mar!

We pretend our fort is a pirate ship.
It's raining on the high seas!

Al poco rato deja de llover.

In a little while, it stops raining.

Salimos a la calle.

We run outside.

17

Mi hermano y yo corremos a los charcos.

My brother and I race to the puddles.

18

Me toca saltar. ¡Splash!

It's my turn to jump in. Splash!

Veo lombrices grandes y gordas en la acera.

I see big, fat worms on the sidewalk.

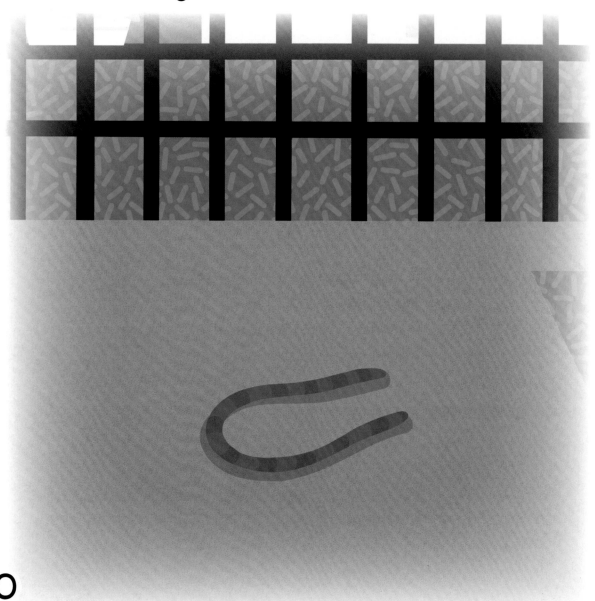

Salen cuando llueve.

They come out when it rains.

21

Pronto empieza a llover otra vez.

Soon it starts raining again.

¡Es hora de entrar!

It's time to go inside!

Palabras que debes aprender
Words to Know

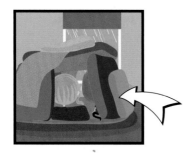

(la) almohada
pillow

(el) charco
puddle

(la) lombriz
worm

Índice / Index

24